CATAMOUNT'S

CATERWAUL

CATAMOUNT'S

CATERWAUL

Faith Van Enk

There once was a great occasion where all the cats were called from out the words where they were hiding to Catamount's great hall.

Cattail came willingly enough with a happy purr and sigh from out the swamp where he had sat watching the butterfly.

Catalog
and
baby Category
first had to
have a
bath.

Catcall came nosily with a sarcastic laugh.

Sleek
and
lovely
Catwalk
walked
a
narrow
way.

leapt

Catapult   the

castle wall

with
fur
all
stoney
gray.

One moved from off a stack of books with sober, strong intent.

Catechism listened to the mighty call and went where he was sent.

astr

Cat   ophe

and

Ca t a c l y sm

l e f tCHAOS

in

their

wake.

Catnip

slowly

got up

with a silly

lazy

quake.

Deep in the earth among the tombs one listened with a sigh. Slowly Catacombs climbed upon her feet and asked a sullen

"Why?"

Catatonic almost did not make it,
see the stare upon his face.

But just in time
Catnap woke up
and *bopped* him in the face.

From out all their hiding
places in the land of
words, the cats came
forth and left behind
something
            rather

                    absurd.

an empty *call* upon a *walk* with *a-pult* and poor *a-chism*.

a *tail*, a *log*, and *e-gor-y* with no one left to quiz him.
Nip was left with *a-combs*, and *a-tonic* sat with *nap*.

a tail   a log   e-gor-y

Nip a-combs

A-TOMIC nap

aclysm
astrophe

And lying in a heap,
astrophe, with *aclysm* in
his lap.

Without their
cats
these words were
left
in quite a
mess.

Stuck
on the page,
unhappy, they will have
to wait,

I guess.

Winding their way the cats came to Catamount's great hall, climbing the stairs they met him upon the rampart's wall.

"Tonight we dine on fishes brought by our friend Catfish."

"The
   lovely
      Cataract
         is pouring
            streams
         of milk
      within
         each
            dish."

"I've called to honor you and the important place you play, without us cats the world of words would surely go astray.

Eat up! Eat up! The night is very young. The world of words must wait for us. The cat has got her tongue!"

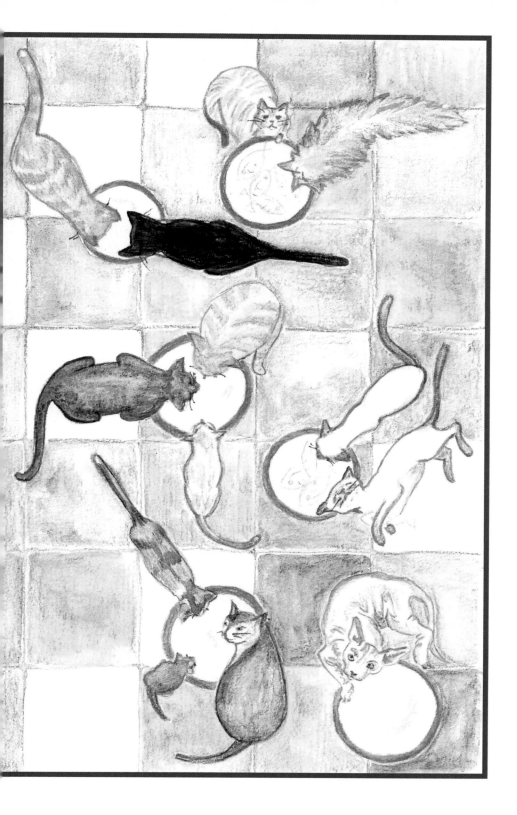

When all
had finished feasting
they climbed
upon the wall,
they faced the moon and
joyfully began their

C A T E R W A U L .

Then slowly they
d
  e
    s
      c
        e
          n
            d
              e
                d
and went back
unto their homes; they
rejoined their broken
words from Catcall to
Catacombs.

Arching his great neck the great catamount ascended and roared one more mighty roar.

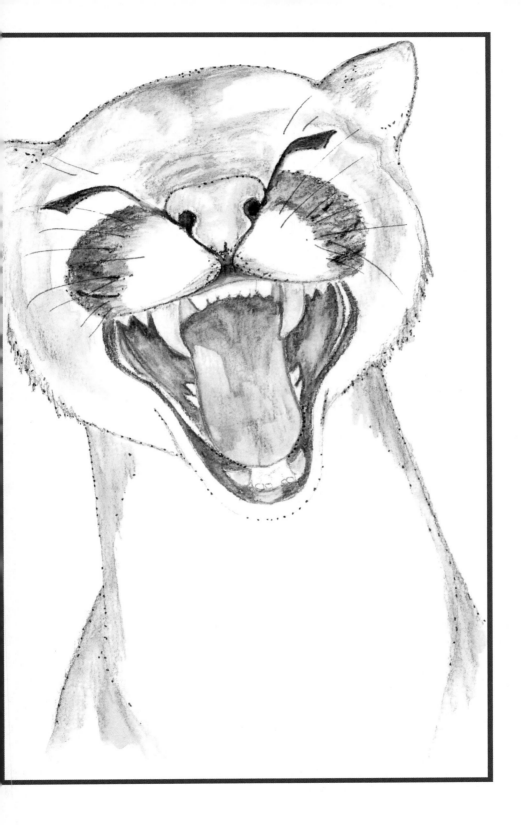

The story now is ended.

Catamount: a large wild cat
Cattail: tall reedy swamp plants with brown furry spikes
Catalog: a book that contains a list of items
Category: a placement of like items
Catcall: a loud mocking call
Catwalk: a narrow walkway
Catapult: an ancient weapon for hurling large stones
Catechism: a book of religious teaching using questions and answers
Catastrophe: a violent destructive event
Cataclysm: a momentous violent event of overwhelming upheaval and demolition
Catacombs: an underground cemetery with many side rooms
Catatonic: staring expression with lack of movement
Catnap: a very short light nap
Catfish: muscular bony fish without scales having long feelers on the head
Cataract: steep rapids in a river or a waterfall
Caterwaul: a loud harsh cry

Made in the USA
Monee, IL
28 December 2020